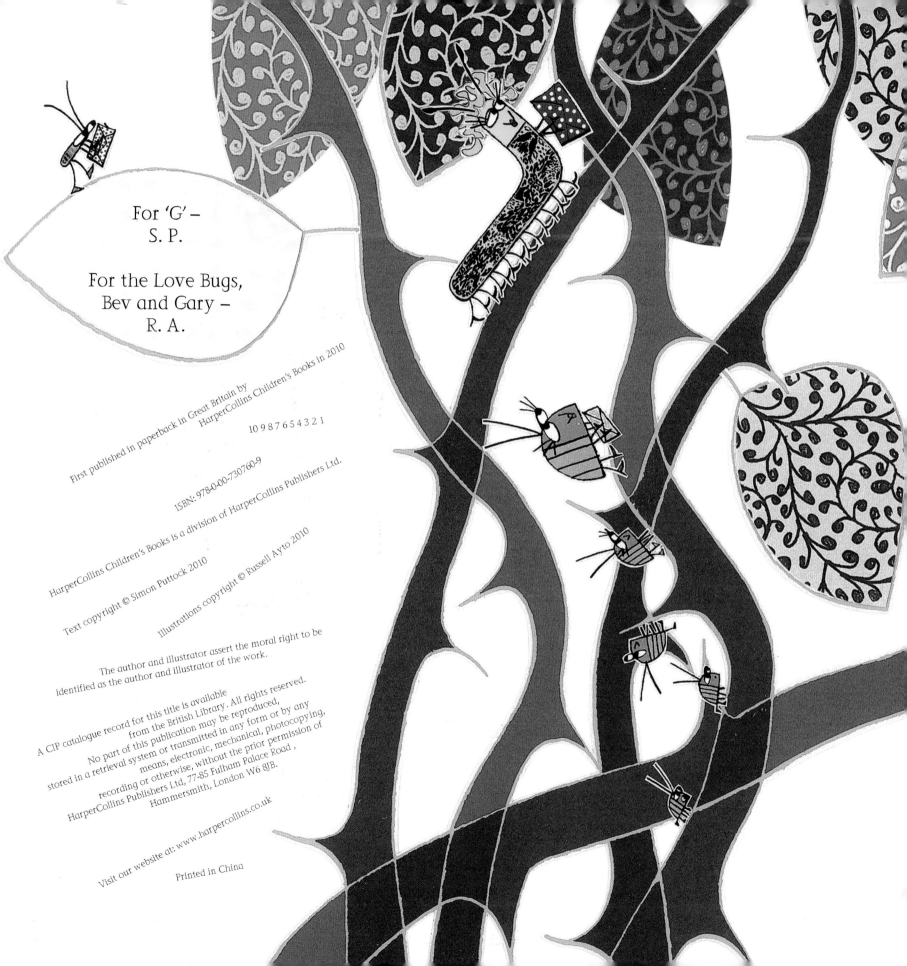

For 'G' –
S. P.

For the Love Bugs,
Bev and Gary –
R. A.

First published in paperback in Great Britain by
HarperCollins Children's Books in 2010

10 9 8 7 6 5 4 3 2 1

ISBN: 978-0-00-730760-9

HarperCollins Children's Books is a division of HarperCollins Publishers Ltd.

Text copyright © Simon Puttock 2010

Illustrations copyright © Russell Ayto 2010

Visit our website at: www.harpercollins.co.uk

Printed in China

THE L♥VE BUGS

Simon Puttock

illustrated by Russell Ayto

HarperCollins *Children's Books*

On Valentine's morning,
all the garden bugs were gathered round
comparing their valentine cards.
Everyone had one, or
two, or MORE.

But Ladybird had **none**.
She sat under a rose bush
feeling sad and **alone**.

Then
all at once
she spied
a most
surprising
thing:

tucked amongst
the petals of a scarlet rose
was an envelope
which said, To 'Red'.

"Well, well!" cried Ladybird,
"I am red! I'm the reddest
thing ever! That must be for me!"
And she opened it at once.

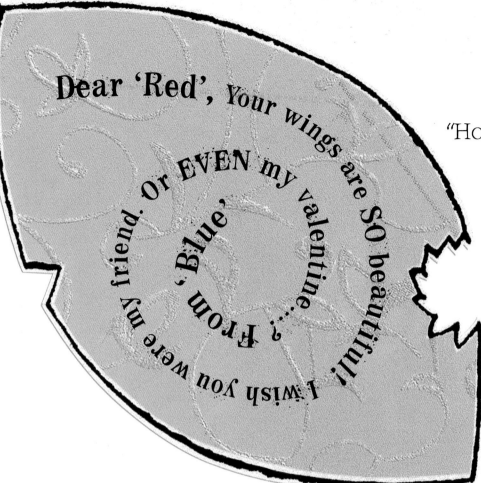

Dear 'Red', Your wings are SO beautiful! I wish you were my friend. Or EVEN my valentine...? From 'Blue'.

Ladybird was overjoyed. "How clever of 'Blue' to notice my wings (I hardly ever unfold them!)

But who IS 'Blue'?"

Ladybird thought hard. "Of course!" she cried. "Dragonfly is very blue, and a fine fellow too!" Ladybird wrote a note immediately, agreeing to everything.

Then she went off to tell her family that Dragonfly **admired** her wings.

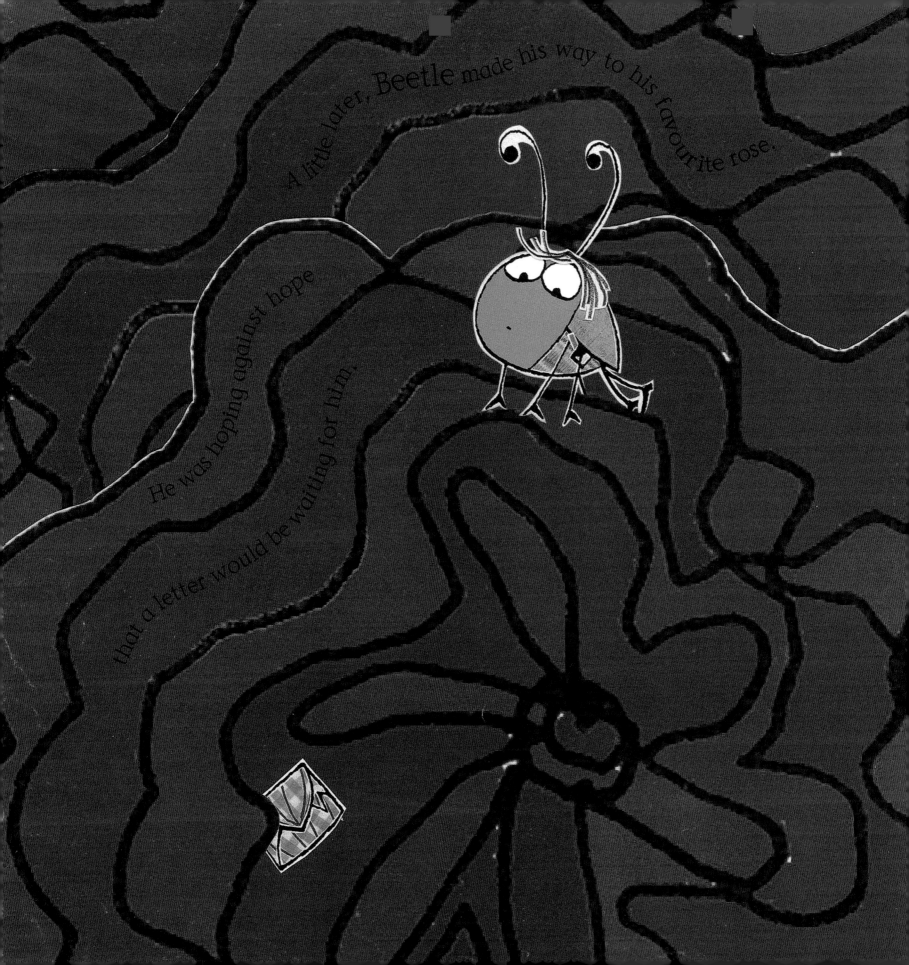

A little later, Beetle made his way to his favourite rose.

He was hoping against hope that a letter would be waiting for him.

"Oh, joy!" he cried when he saw the note, and he sat down on a buttercup to read it.

Dear 'Blue',
I am SO glad you like my wings.
I WILL be your valentine.
From 'Red'

Beetle's heart **filled** with happiness! He wrote another letter...

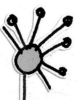

and dashed
home to tell **his**
family that he
was in

love.

Ladybird was nervous
as she made her way back
to the rose bush.
What if there
was no reply?

But, "Oh, delight!" she cried when she saw the letter.

DEAREST 'Red'!
You have made me the
happiest bug in the world!
Let me say I LOVE you?
Longingly,
'Blue'

Ladybird blushed as red as the
rose. "He loves me," she cried
and she wrote a reply.

Then she hurried
home to her family
and announced
that she was
practically
engaged.

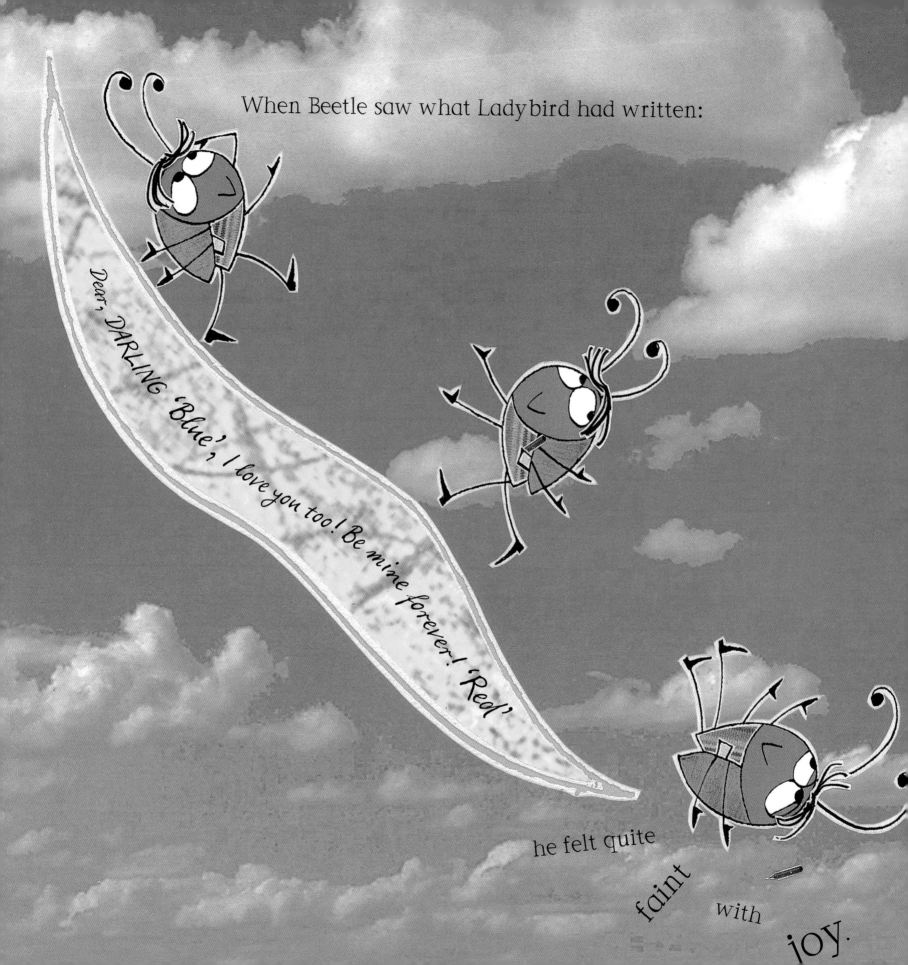

When Beetle saw what Ladybird had written:

Dear, DARLING 'Blue', I love you too! Be mine forever! 'Red'

he felt quite faint with joy.

It was all he could do to scribble:

My own, true 'Red', I WILL, I mean I AM, I DO, so marry me tonight upon this very rose at moon rise! From 'Blue'

When Ladybird read **that** letter, she could hardly contain her excitement.

She wrote a **great big**

Yes!

X at the bottom, and flew all the way home.

"MAMA!" she screamed. "Make me a wedding dress right this minute...

...for

I am

going to be

married!"

That night,

everyone gathered

at the rose bush

to see the happy couple wed.

Moth had kindly
agreed to perform
the ceremony.

"Now, son," said Beetle's father as they waited patiently upon a petal, "are you SURE she is everything you say she is? We have not even met the girl, you know."

"Oh," sighed Beetle,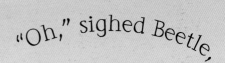

"she is everything and more!"

"Now, daughter," said Ladybird's
mother as they climbed up to the rose,
"are you sure he is everything you say he is?
We know so little about him."

"Oh," sighed Ladybird, "he is

everything

and more!"

But alas, when the moon rose,

and Ladybird saw Beetle...

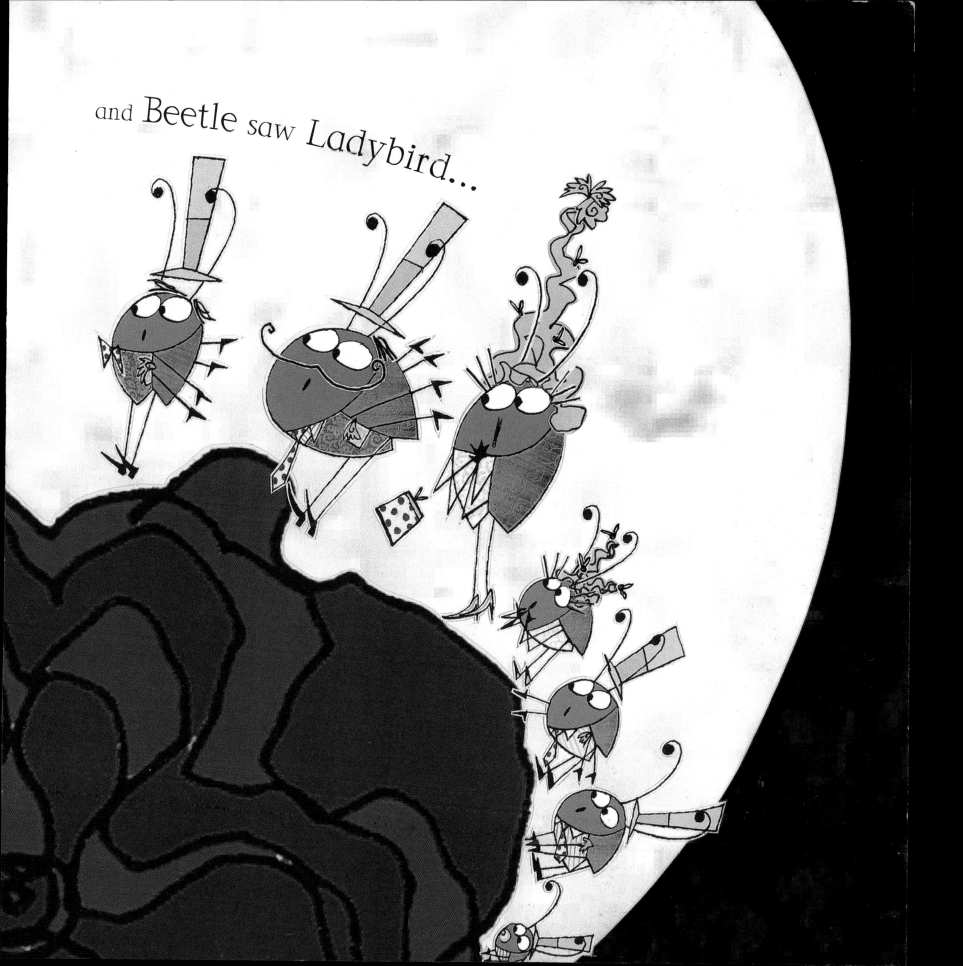

and Beetle saw Ladybird...

"I am here to marry Dragonfly,"
said Ladybird.

"And I am here
to marry Butterfly,"
said Beetle.

"Oh dear,"

said Moth.

"Oh dear,

oh dear,

oh dear."

Ladybird gave a little scream

and spread her wings...

and

flew

to a

distant

leaf

to be

alone.

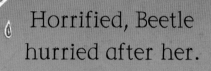

Horrified, Beetle
hurried after her.

"Oh, go away!"
said Ladybird,
"I feel like such
a fool!"

But Beetle did not go away.

Instead he wrote

another note:

Dear 'Red'
(meaning Ladybird),
I feel like a fool too.
But your wings really ARE
very fine, and close up,
you are even more beautiful
than Butterfly. I don't think we
ought to be married tonight, but won't
you be my UNEXPECTED valentine?
From 'Blue'

(as in Beetle)

Ladybird wiped away her tears.

"Oh, Beetle," she sighed,

"you do write such wonderful letters!

And now that I look at you properly, you are every bit as fine as Dragonfly, so yes, I will be your valentine – If you will be mine."

And Ladybird gave Beetle her hand, and there in the moon-shadowed garden...

they **danced**
with each other
(quite smoochily)
till dawn.